Lullaby Babes

Maribeth Boelts

Illustrations by Don Sullivan

ALBERT WHITMAN & COMPANY • MORTON GROVE, ILLINOIS

Text typeface:Weidemann Bold.
Illustration media: watercolor and colored pencil.
Designer: Karen Johnson Campbell.

Text copyright © 1995 by Maribeth Boelts.
Illustrations copyright © 1995 by Don Sullivan.
Published in 1995 by Albert Whitman & Company,
6340 Oakton Street, Morton Grove, Illinois 60053-2723.
Published simultaneously in Canada
by General Publishing, Limited, Toronto.
Printed in the United States of America.
10 9 8 7 6 5 4 3 2 1

Library of Congress Cataloging-in-Publication Data

Boelts, Maribeth, 1964-
Lullaby babes / written by Maribeth Boelts; illustrated by Don Sullivan.
p.   cm.
Summary: A series of poems which present various mother animals
singing to their babies ends with a human mother and child.
ISBN 0-8075-4792-1
[1. Animals—Infancy—Fiction. 2. Babies—Fiction.
3. Lullabies—Fiction. 4. Stories in rhyme.]
I. Sullivan, Don, ill. II. Title.
PZ8.3.B599545Lu 1995   95-1319
[E]—dc20   CIP
                                                                    AC

To Adam, Hannah, and Will, and to my mother. M.B.
To N. J. for the countless hours of lullabies. D.S.

*M*ama dove with her tiny one
on a rafter in the barn,
softly now—the day is through—
sings her babe a lulla-coo.

*Mama cat in a cardboard box,
five new kittens by her side,
tenderly, she cleans their fur,
sings her babes a lulla-purr.*

In the pond, now dark and still,
Mama trout with her silver young,
keeps them from all kinds of trouble,
sings her babes a lulla-bubble.

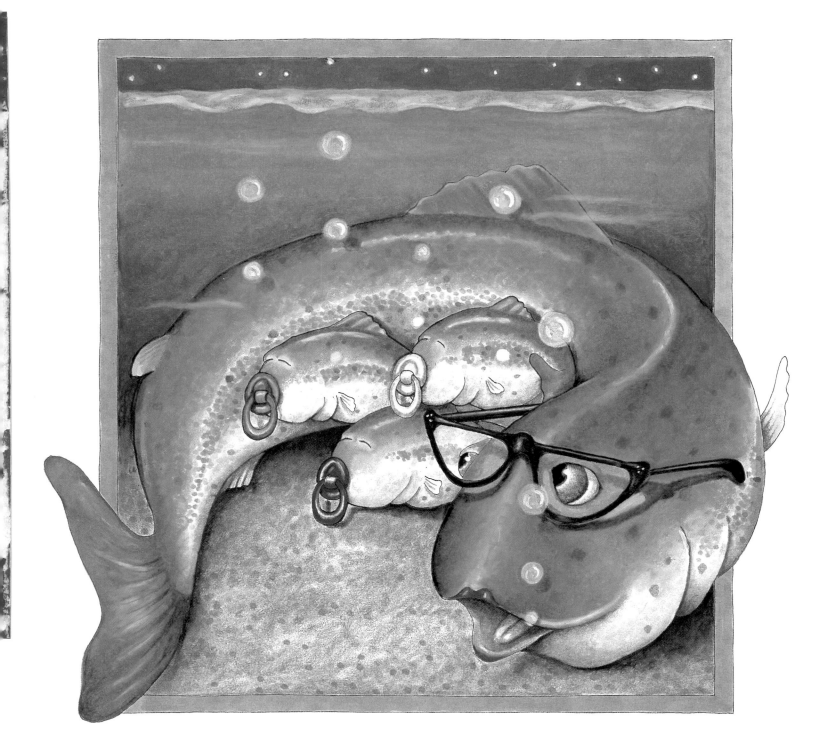

In the oak tree on the hill,
Mama owl keeps watch at night,
happy with her feathered two,
sings her babes a lulla-whoo.

Mama sow in a corner pen,
six fat piglets, bellies full,
finds some room for the left-out runt,
sings her babes a lulla-grunt.

*In the shadows of their stall,
Mama horse, with restless colt,
makes a bed in the soft, warm hay,
sings her babe a lulla-neigh.*

Mama cow with her day-old calf,
wobbly on his brand-new legs.
She nuzzles him as mamas do,
sings her babe a lulla-moo.

Underneath a fallen branch,
Mama mouse's work is done.
She can't resist one last proud peek,
sings her babes a lulla-squeak.

*Mama white sheep, baby black
snuggle close, a cozy pair.
They share a treat as gentle Ma
sings her babe a lulla-baa.*

In the bedroom of the child,
Mama and her loved one rock.
Mama gazes at the sky,
sings her babe a lullaby.

Lullaby Babes

Lyrics by Maribeth Boelts
Music by Judith Mathews

Moderato, playful

Dm · C · Dm · Am

Ma - ma dove with her ti - ny one on a raf - ter in the barn,

Dm · C · Dm · Dm A Dm

soft - ly now — the day is through — sings her babe a lul - la - coo.